CACOPHONY

CACOPHONY

COLLECTED SHORT STORIES

VOLUME ONE

BY BP GREGORY

COPYRIGHT © 2013 BP GREGORY

ALL RIGHTS RESERVED

ALL RIGHTS RESERVED. This work is copyright apart from any use permitted under the Copyright Act 1968. This work may not be reproduced or transmitted in part or in its entirety in any form or by any means, electronic or mechanical, including photocopying, recording, or by any information storage and retrieval system, nor may any other exclusive right be exercised, without the prior written consent of the author BP Gregory, except where permitted by law.

This is a work of fiction. Places and place names are either fictional, or used fictitiously. Any resemblance to persons either living or dead is purely co-incidental.

This is the Second Edition.

ISBN 978 0 6458265 4 8

Content Advisory

These stories feature adult themes including abuse, cannibalism, claustrophobia, graphic violence/gore, loss of a loved one, mental health issues, sexually explicit scenes, traumatic death, vehicular accident, and war. They may not be suitable for all readers.

Acknowledgments

Cacophony cover image by ollyy. Promise cover image by Karramba Production. What a View cover image by Matthew Benoit. Follow cover image by Suzanne Tucker. Drive cover image by panco971. Commitment cover image by Mayer George. The Man's Heart cover image by bergamont. It's All About the Love cover image by Christy Liem. The Elevator Story cover image by Norman Chan. All courtesy of Shutterstock.

Something for Everything cover image by Extradeda, The Town cover images by Pavelr and Tim Bird, Abstract cover image by Pete Sherrard, Orotund cover image by Alex Malikov, and Visit the Website image by Peter Dedeurwaerder all courtesy of Shutterstock.

What a View was first published in print in 2004 as part of All Change Please, Cardigan Press' collection of short experimental fiction.

The Man's Heart was first released in 2004 as part of G Wells Taylor's ezine The Wildclown Chronicle.

It's All About The Love was first released in 2004 as part of G Wells Taylor's ezine The Wildclown Chronicle.

STORIES

Copyright	v
Content Advisory	vii
Acknowledgments	ix
Promise	1
What a View	13
Follow	25
Drive	31
Commitment	39
The Man's Heart	53
It's All About the Love	61
The Elevator Story	67
Abstract (special bonus short story)	83

PROMISE

BP GREGORY

PROMISE

Crossing four lanes to the café, Guntarc's friend was indistinguishable from the downpour until traffic was already on her. A spray of horns and bright commuter panic broke on the woman's weary indifference. She seemed to wash up on the pavement ok.

No observer would believe that in their teens that same figure had dandied about dressed like gay pride come early. Hell, Guntarc thought; what were we even going to be, back then? Top of the dollar school with dutifully attended seminars on leadership, promises of glory, but not a single damn course gave tips on how you coped ending up just like everyone else. Now *that* would have been an education.

The door banged, dispersing nostalgia's thick fug and Guntarc raised his hand—classroom days again! His friend saw and brought the weather squeezing across to the table like a wet dog.

This café was counter-service country; but obstinately bringing the mountain to Mohammed was a war the friend had won many times before. The café's staff merited even less of a nod from her than they gave. They'd come around.

She contorted free of a bedraggled chrysalis of bag, gloves and a dangerously long scarf that threatened to snag a travelator and twist her head off someday. Finally divested, she then perched herself opposite with the skittishness of a woman who was stealing this sip of time. 'Well look at the state of you.'

And this was what he got *after* serious efforts to scrape things together.

'Wild night?'

Piqued, Guntarc placed his mobile phone down on the laminate between them with a faint grinding click.

His friend dabbled nervously in the spilled sweetener. 'Not this again! Seriously, Guntarc I. Did not. Call you last night. At all!' She tried for forcefulness, sweeping grains away. 'Really, I get enough crazy already from my two year old.'

'That's interesting. Although by interesting I mean a big pile of crap. You see, I went and recorded it this time.'

The cushion beneath her sighed out its mustiness. His friend had cringed back as though rather than offering the phone he had lunged in to stab her with it. Sighing, he slipped it away in his pocket.

'You really ought to listen to it. Look—we both know something's not right!' Guntarc stopped with difficulty and ratcheted himself down a level at her nervous, irritable gesture. They were attracting dull curiosity around the café. 'Just *listen* to it. You sound hysterical.'

'Just something saucy the hubby and I enjoy at home,' she tried weakly. 'Don't judge us.'

'Nice try. Your Peter was all tucked up and snoring right where he should be, but you weren't there. Where do you go in the night when everyone thinks you're asleep? Where are you calling me from, crying and whispering that you can't breathe and I have to come save you?'

Rage and resignation were having a hard time coming to terms on her sparse, pale mouth. There wasn't enough to work with. 'My neighbours are going to have your ass hauled off by the cops one day for sneaking about my roof in the middle of the damned night. And that's assuming you don't put a foot wrong and break your damned neck first.'

'Fear of falling's never been my thing,' he said smugly.

'I know, what do you think scares *me* so much? And why not just knock on the door and wake Pete, like any other paranoid fruitcake?'

'Because …'

Because you called *me*. Not him. He was right there, and you called me!

She rolled her eyes. 'Don't you see? It's because Pete would prove you're hallucinating, that I'm right where I belong, and "poof!" goes your weird conspiracy theory. Face it Guntarc. You need more excitement in your life.'

He leaned forward. 'My bird's ready to fly.'

'Oh no—I take it back!'

'Seeing how you had me out of bed last night anyhow …'

'I did not!'

'… I thought what the hell and pulled an all-nighter. I've *finished* that beautiful bastard.'

'You haven't been to bed at all? Coffee won't keep you going forever.'

'Long enough …'

With a fine instinct for poor timing, the café barista had crept up to sulk at Guntarc's elbow. He was a *barista*. He shouldn't have to wait tables!

Ignoring the kid's martyrdom Guntarc's friend caught at

his slat-like arm. 'Hey. What would you say if I told you that someone had built an *airplane* in their garage?'

Bright, childlike wonder shone, for a moment. Just as hastily shrouded, but that glimpse of the stars made even this baseline specimen of humanity momentarily beautiful.

The barista responded slowly. 'Wouldn't people notice?'

'A small one.'

He chewed his lip anxiously as though they'd be recording his answer. 'Ordinary people can't fly. *Terrorists* fly. And the police, to catch them. If there really were an airplane somebody would have told the cops by now. You guys want coffee?'

The friend leaned back with satisfaction, as though she'd proven some critical point. 'Black, strong. Two muffins and a cookie.' The café's warm yeasty air had driven her to extravagance. 'Guntarc?'

'Sure; one more top-up won't kill me.' He was little more than caffeine and nervous twitches anyhow, had that look like nobody'd ever fed him.

The barista was off and back quicker than it took to do the job right, but whatever the quality the drinks were still heartblood going down. Chipped saucers rattled on the table.

Guntarc bridled impatiently until their new mate had re-established himself back at his machine, safe beyond earshot. The kid's face had lost its dull slackness of expression, become thoughtful.

'Ten bucks says that little weed won't be sleeping tonight. You should start an insomnia club.'

'Huh?'

'You can't go around giving people the suspicion that there might be something out there beyond the next wage packet or a nice shiny bauble. It's a sickness of society, that kind of thinking.'

'Why can't you take nice girls out on dates, instead of sitting up all night in your garage? Take your mind off things.'

'You meet a girl who wants to hang out in my garage without getting me arrested, you let me know.' He shifted in his seat. 'Are you coming tonight? I reckon the rain will give me my best chance at staying hidden; it's like the skies want me up there.'

'Guntarc, a thousand monkeys could not describe my lack of interest in watching you kill yourself.'

Blunt fingers rasped across his chin. 'I'm not doing this for suicide. Nobody says I *have* to die.'

'But you *could!* You probably will! Why do it?'

'Because!' He was just as exasperated. 'Because I can! Because they shouldn't make people not want to! They shouldn't keep us scared all the time.'

She glared and their afternoon could have gone south, but then she burst out laughing. 'Just once it would be nice to get together and just chat. Why do we always have to squabble?'

'We don't have much in common anymore, I guess.'

His friend threw her hands up sarcastically, never imagining he meant it. 'Then why stay friends?'

'Because you're the only person who remembers what I might have been. The last one in the world. And I do the same for you. Hell, I need that just to get through the day.'

There was a long disbelieving silence. 'That is a whole new level of asshole even for you.'

'I know.'

'I'm busy living a normal, *responsible* life! Just like everybody! We can't all be hippies and radicals, and … and …'

Guntarc set down his cup. 'I know. Just come and see me fly. I'm going to do something real for once. I want you there.'

'No chance! I'm not stirring one foot to enable your nonsense.' The friend struggled with her natural reticence, chipped nails skittering about her cup … but what if he meant it? 'You can't do this. You *can't*. What will I do when you're gone?'

He had to avert his face from the weary, hopelessness in hers.

'Something,' he muttered. 'Hopefully something.'

Guntarc's nonsense stayed with the friend all that day, skewing routine's grey sameness into something frightening.

'Nonsense,' she repeated to herself while preparing for bed that evening in her neat pantomime house. A comfortable home with everything in its place including Pete, who was already droning away, lost to the world. Poor Pete's job was a nightmare and he was constantly too exhausted to be bothered by much of anything.

The friend couldn't afford to be getting about with any of Guntarc's insanity! Look at how far she and Pete were stretched already just to meet what ends had to be tied. It was ridiculous! Just like the tether binding her ankle to the bedpost, which was the new technique she hoped would keep her safely abed all night. Mostly it worked. "Disturbing" could not describe how it felt to wake up with black earth between her toes. Or sometimes her nightdress missing. Or all her fingernails broken.

Usually snuggling into her husband's prosaic farting warmth made everything better, but tonight the friend rocked fretfully on the bed's cold lonely edge. Time went plunging uncontrollably by, like the icy raindrops beyond the fogged-up window. It was all nonsense, and of course Guntarc would chicken out anyhow. Ordinary people couldn't fly.

What the friend's eyes refused to witness imagination tormented her with; twice as vividly. The bird would take to the air. She'd never known Guntarc to back down from a challenge.

Holding herself in the lonely bedroom she saw sinister dark choppers arise in Guntarc's wake, obscuring the beautiful stars. Oily mini guns spinning up beside the all-important camera: the avid public eye had to watch hubris cut down, the lesson of that flaming wreckage hurled from the heavens.

But just this once Guntarc never looked back. The cruel wind cut streamers of water from his reddened eyes.

Hands sure on the controls Guntarc flew on into the night and finally his heart cried joy, joy!

From the Author

A little about the story:
Promise began with a single red light, blinking threateningly on an answering machine. That sense of deep seated dread before you press the button.

A talented mate of mine, Tim Egan, was writing a fascinating and darksome film script, but had hit a wall when his female character kept calling her friend in terror to tell him … what? So *my* friend asked me to see what I could make of the premise. Tim and I had both recently graduated from a rather prestigious house of learning; thrust out the front doors stuffed full of lessons on how to succeed, lead, conquer. Go go go!

What I felt we students were lacking were the more modest skills on how to fail. That vital technique of picking yourself up off the pavement, dusting down your pride and carrying on; and all this frustration came spilling out in the short piece I penned.

As so often happens, when I presented Promise it was useless for Tim's purposes, but I quite liked it and went on to develop it into a short. I was later thrilled to find that people HAVE and continue to build small, light aircraft in their garages—sometimes hidden from the neighbours. Who knows what could be going on next door?

The pieces of Guntarc and the friend's lives continue in another short story called Stow, published 2014 and available as part of Orotund: Collected Short Stories Volume Two.

What a View

BP GREGORY

WHAT A VIEW

THE BILLBOARD WAS leviathan, and you'd assume an affront to the jolly vacationing of x-hundred busy-bee consumers. At least eighty percent of prime sunny coast had no hope of glimpsing the sea until they stood ankle deep in it, sand down their butt cracks and salt in their eyes.

However, never underestimate the public's craving for leisure. They blithely continued to glut their collective maw with dairy-free confectionery and shell jewellery, and enjoy their seaside holiday regardless.

A bullet, a freakin' *bullet* whanged the corroded metal beside my head.

As though this monstrosity didn't sway enough, the ballistics set the billboard's whole iron-mix superstructure humming until my bones vibrated in sympathy. Prehistoric lattice whined its complaint right through my skull. Oh dear Lord please don't look down! My heart choked convulsively, trying to drag both lungs around itself.

Bullets were too much. Luckily they weren't trying to nail me with anything more up-market for fear of damaging my perch. This overgrown postcard was the most coveted chunk of skyline anywhere, ever. And my advertisement, my very own baby, conceived under contract for Aspens beer, sprawled luxuriously across it.

The main highlight drew your eye down the long curving arc of a man's spine, sinuous and sinewy. No face (or the cleft peach of men's peculiar flat buttocks, which could be just as distinguishing), just this lovely depersonalised back. Muscled, and yet touchingly defenceless. It made you want to lay him flat and just bathe the entire expanse with your tongue.

The product, hardly there by comparison, was rendered more perfectly than any bottle of Aspens could actually be. But more importantly, better than any competing beer *would* be. You'd suck it down, look at the billboard and think wistfully, Gee, I wish that had been an Aspens. Aspens had purchased the longest megaspace run to date, longest by a full thirty-two seconds. The grotesque outlay could probably have bought all competitors outright.

Thirty-two seconds would have been enough to put Aspens unfairly ahead. By my watch, I had now kept the Aspens billboard nude alive for a further four hours and counting.

I clutched my rifle, palm gummy with hot sweat and machine grease. The digits looked too refined for the job. They curled, embarrassed, the pinkie breaking ranks to salute high in the air. My other arm had accepted the practicalities of the situation and was trying to become one with the T-brace behind me. Sirens and the complaints of nearby gulls mingled eerily in the air.

Super. Somebody was climbing the scaffolding again. Mighty flat learning curve these people exhibited. I readied the gun.

'Wait!'

White cotton flopped limply. It looked like some kindly citizen below had donated their t-shirt, entranced enough by the drama to go cold in the breeze. I lowered my rifle.

The man struggling his way up the maintenance ladder was a suit. Although young, he looked born to wear ties and pressed slacks. Likely squeezed into the world bloody and squalling with expensive silk already collaring his chubby little neck. Although to his credit, when I first got so high up the billboard all I'd wanted was to vomit helplessly and then fall off, while he seemed inclined to do neither.

I wiped my hand before offering it. There was grit everywhere, the metal's oxidisation stirred about by every breath of wind coming in off the sea. I'd seen the water bloody with it around the pylons, carmine seaweed swirling backward and forward. Tiny scarlet fish had darted in and out of its protection, rocked by the swell.

My skin and scalp itched fiercely. I must look like some mad, ochre-daubed tribeswoman, and grimaced to complete the picture. 'Meredith.'

A suit's impersonal handshake. 'Andrew. You can call me last hope, though. I'm from Anglesea Chips.' He shuffled ultra-lat learning curve these people exhibited. I readied the gun.

'Wait!'

White cotton flopped limply. It looked like some kindly citizen below had donated their t-shirt, entranced enough by the drama to go cold in the breeze. I lowered my rifle.

The man struggling his way up the maintenance ladder was a suit. Although young, he looked born to wear ties and pressed slacks. Likely squeezed into the world bloody and squalling with expensive silk already collaring his chubby little neck.

Although to his credit, when I first got so high up the billboard all I'd wanted was to vomit helplessly and then fall off, while he seemed inclined to do neither.

I wiped my hand before offering it. There was grit everywhere, the metal's oxidisation stirred about by every breath of wind coming in off the sea. I'd seen the water bloody with it around the pylons, carmine seaweed swirling backward and forward. Tiny scarlet fish had darted in and out of its protection, rocked by the swell.

My skin and scalp itched fiercely. I must look like some mad, ochre-daubed tribeswoman, and grimaced to complete the picture. 'Meredith.'

A suit's impersonal handshake. 'Andrew. You can call me last hope, though. I'm from Anglesea Chips.' He shuffled ultra-g gloss shoes fastidiously, shaking a rain of ruddy flakes loose, and glanced at his wristwatch. Copious jet-black hair poked and curled from under the chrome band, like he kept a second pubis hidden beneath those cufflinks. Holding that cool palm, I tried to imagine his back's contours behind the prison of all that tailoring. Probably the hair rooted at the nape of his neck ran all the way down to meet that ascending from his crack.

'Ms Meredith, we don't have a lot of time here. Aspens have hit the denial button, but I for one didn't come down in the last shower. How much are they paying you?'

Despite myself I grinned, the sort of little smirk that just comes creeping round the edges and you can't take back. 'What can you prove, Mr Andrew? There's a lot of money involved. After all, Aspens will only ever have to buy this publicity once. Even if you Anglesea lads could pull a stunt this big, you'd only be a copy. I am the first.'

'Your "stunt", as you put it, is ruining lives. Seventeen companies on average go broke for every second Aspens is up here; why do you think billboard time is so valuable? Projections say that if this ad endures, in thirty-six minutes Aspens will control two thirds of *everything*.'

The suit was sure sweating up a storm, the rattle of his words like hail in a bucket. His sweetish man-odour reached even my rust-clogged nose. Nobody had ever pitched their case so fast.

'Ms Meredith, you can't seriously believe the world's prepared to bend over and take that. They've got some pretty serious action planned to stop you reaching that thirty-six minute event horizon.'

'You don't represent Anglesea Chips,' I said decisively.

'Well no, you couldn't strictly say I'm "representing" them right now. This is a big opportunity for the both of us.' The suit checked his watch again, compulsively. Doubtless he straightened the paintings at home in a flat full of geometrically aligned furniture. 'I'll sign you a sweet deal, on behalf of the company of course, who will thoroughly reward me. You get to avoid living out your youth in a jail cell with Big Bertha. The story of how you got paid to flush your life away takes down Aspens forever, and we are both stars.'

'Your company had the billboard booked for this timeslot.' I smiled. 'Anglesea could only afford sixteen minutes.'

His teeth gnashed (another peek at the watch). 'It's now or never. I'm the only one willing to help. Aspens won't protect you.'

'In a little while Aspens will be able to do whatever they want. They're part of consumer consciousness by now, as accepted as gravity and air. Nobody can buy beer ... nobody will ever drink *anything* again without thinking of this whopping great product idol. Eventually they won't survive without it.'

'You're crazy if you think ...'

A heavy *whumping* drowned out the suit's protest, and brought a sickly horrified gleam to his eyes.

'No!' He tapped the face of his watch, shook it. 'It's too early!' The ponderous air compressions grew louder. He dropped his white rag and, wrenching off the watch, hurled it out into space in an impotent over-arm throw. Black goaty hairs still caught in the band. 'Stupid slow piece of shit!'

Cheese-coloured, he flung himself back down the ladder. A gibbered litany of curses drifted back to me. I kicked the flag off the edge and it overtook his descent, twisting and falling like a boneless dead gull.

Whump, whump. What rose to my view were a series of matte-black helicopters, their blind nose cones pointed unerringly to the billboard and myself, a tiny clinging speck on its side, staring. A black armoured line of helicopters that marched away to both horizons. My hair blew out behind me in the stinking hurricane of their exhaust.

Disbelief locked my hands around the rifle, fat lot of good it would do me now. They couldn't do this! Surely not: the billboard was too valuable, and ... and my *ad*.

I looked down and saw that the ambitious suit who'd tried to make a name for himself was not going to make it either. Bet he didn't see this day coming when he bought such a shitty watch.

Oh crap. I didn't even know if this would kill Aspens, or merely make them stronger. The public was about to see their fledgling god become a warping molten ball, see it rain girders onto the faithful below, and then tip backward and fall into the sea. Some wouldn't survive. Already habituated to the ad's place in their universe, they would smash open Aspens bottles to shred their eyes and wrists on the shards. Die stinking of beer, immersed in that special back-alley-of-a-pub sort of smell.

The helicopters fired with synchronicity only computers could manage. The derisive hiss of rockets. Dolphin-slim, their tails an expanding bloom of fire.

Quick, I tried to think of one last nice thing, a beautiful thought to have before I died, but my heart was hammering in my ears too loudly. The thick rust in my mouth tasted like crap. I didn't want to die with a mouthful of that. All I could think was: I hope it doesn't hurt. It shocked me that I couldn't imagine one nice thing.

I looked up at the billboard, that inhumanly lovely arc of skin that I wanted to put my mouth on.

And then.

From the Author

A little about the story:
What a View was my submission to All Change Please, Cardigan Press' collection of Fast Fiction for Any Trip: a collection of short stories cleverly sorted by length so you can have exactly the right read to suit your commute. I was so very thrilled when it got in, and if you've never read any of Cardigan Press' little bundles of joy don't be shy to pick one up.

The fashion at the time seemed to be for very serious, beautiful cultural diaspora-type stories, with little ese being taken "seriously," but high-brow was hardly my schtick. I wanted to express my love of the exessive, of helicopters, extremity, and things that went bang!

I hadn't even realised that Cardigan Press were already putting together collections of quirky, cutting edge Australian fiction until it was pointed out to me, and that discovery was like coming home.

FOLLOW

BP GREGORY

FOLLOW

Mary's desiccated white hands with their poor ragged nails clung comfortingly to each other. It wasn't much, but they'd never managed to hold on to anything else.

'Here Mare!' Joe's false joviality, his voice grating like stone. 'Poppin' up all over like mushrooms, these are!'

'Alive?' It was a foolish wish; *fool* she berated herself.

'Dead as my boot.' Joe cackled and then winced, despising the idiot twist of his own tongue. 'They's always ready-dead-dead a'fore the bogeyman gets 'em.'

Mary ground her teeth, swollen gums throbbing. Joe would persist! Some years back he had dropped into dialect and now stubbornly refused to emerge.

As for himself, even more fleshless than Mary from nerves and nicotine Joe lingered three short paces behind her shoulder and watched the wind snatching her loose hair back and forth, as though he had nowhere better to be in the world. He had every coarse strand down to memory by now. Mary wore her hair down to shelter her ears but they looked ruddy and sore anyhow, poor things.

'I hear talk goin' about, you know. Little gossips say it's the bogeyman all right. Some folk are reckoning we ought t' leave the cold boys out all night, stop 'im come peepin' 'round for the live ones.'

'Joe, just please grow up.' In Mary's opinion which was practical if not book learned, with the number of wrinkles between them neither had any business trembling over boggarts.

She knelt by Joe's find on mud whipped up by the wind and frozen into peaks and whorls. Joints clicked and groaned all the way down.

They had found death, but it was certainly not mortality that had Joe shying like a nervy horse. With technology exhausted the world had long fallen back on the tradition of cramming war with the fine bodies of its youth: the horizon choked on cadavers so far as the watering eye could see.

Only, *this* boy's clothing and limbs were in disarray. As she stooped over him Mary had to admit that his buttocks, shock white from life's departure, did indeed look like mushrooms pointing at the sleet sky. The same glacial wind making her nose run slashed at those little half-globes but it was skin that would never gooseflesh again.

That sloping curve from shoulder to back was what Mary loved best, all of a man's strength and fragility sketched in a single line. However when she leaned forward, perhaps to stroke those tender knobbles of spine, a sheaf of her own gunmetal grey hair dropped between the body and her avid eyes.

She withdrew, trembling. It was funny how wilful imagination still pictured her hair as brown, as though it were still tumbling on her shoulders like dark chocolate.

'Gossip is ignorant by nature and you oughtn't to go repeating it. It's a man that's doing this.' Only a man, she repeated to herself.

'Humph. Bet if this poor lad could still talk he'd call it the bogeyman, right 'nough. Well help me cover 'im girl! Ain't decent to gawp at a lad with 'is strides down.'

Ever the efficient crow Mary began emptying the dead soldier's pockets of trinkets which rattled around the bottom of her basket. Chapped fingers lingered on stiff green wool. Joe could barely hear her murmur above the wind. 'My man wore a coat like this.'

Green wool kept carefully brushed when it could be and nobody could tend it but her man, sitting patiently by the hour. Buttons that were buffed to a proud mirror sheen at their centre even if the edges stayed irredeemably pitted with rust.

Everything that Mary had ever known of warmth, comfort and pleasure was wrapped tenderly in the memory of her man's skin and the mustiness of green wool. Little wonder following his death she'd failed to leave. Where was she to go?

The back of the bent woman's neck and what little Joe could see of her cheek glowed as though defying the wind. Yet her hands twisting in the coat remained so frail; chalk fingers. He gnawed his cheek and busied himself trying to yank the little soldier's pants back up, but with limited success. The cold had made a marble statue out of the lad.

Still her fiery cheek was ablaze, enough to melt the frozen slush and sink them both. Fond memory stayed fresh, forever young and waxing only more perfect with the years while Joe cracked and gnarled like a footnote left out in the rain.

'Can't we lay him at rest, somehow?' Grey hair and all, forlorn Mary still sounded just like a girl to him.

Joe's bowstring shoulders shrugged, and, 'Th' boy's an icypole,' fell off his tongue before he could halt it.

Mary winced as the wind whistled keenly through her hollowed breast. Were it not for her companion's disapproval she would have liked to put the dead boy's green coat on, to feel its heavy weight wrapped around her like arms.

Her man had been so warm. Even beneath his coat his body had burned like flame, feeding her greedy hands. Some nights the lost ghost of it was such agony that she bit her cheek against crying out, in great crystallised sobs, for him to pity her and bring his warmth back. And not for the first time she thought, this is hell. What drove the bogeyman to come here, to press himself against something so cold and unyielding?

Behind her Joe was quietly stripping the jacket from another body; a colourless garment without memory, the same exhausted grey as the horizon. He wanted to take Mary's painfully thin elbow and help her off the bitter ground, but he knew better. Joe had not seen Mary's face for years. She may not even have a face, only the bowed features of a neck and cold bloodless ears. He could only follow along behind.

'Come on Mare. Everything that c'n be done to the poor lad's already well an' truly done.'

And to us as well.

Joe twisted the oily, cloud-coloured cloth through lumpy fingers but Mary's head only sank lower, her long hair falling down. So he jerked the boy's coat from her white hands and roughly covered the green wool up with grey.

DRIVE

THE GUARD RAIL had gone, flown off into the scrub somewhere and green weeds lay smashed flat by the red car's passage. An indicator winked at me suggestively through its cracked casing.

And I'm sorry to be crude but Jesus; the kid had punched clear through his fly! Silvery threads ran everywhere, a Pro Hart spatter on the speedometer's incriminating face. A desperate ejector reflex, last ditch effort to share his middle class DNA with the world. I resisted a niggling urge to dip a gnawed fingernail in and taste it.

I remember that back in the old days Johnny-boy's issue was sour, a bit nasty and gag-inducing. He would gasp that I was the first ever to swallow it, like I had touched his damned soul. Perhaps that's why he married me. It later negotiated a merger with my body, John's sourness, and made my Becky.

But this boy—no woman would choke his 'wurst now, love it and become his wife. Look at his ride! Slung right to the blacktop, as low as his jeans (with the obligatory white shorts peeping out the top). Custom sprayed a man-whore red, as bright and hard as a cock crow. Collision came free in every millimetre of design. I can picture him now, exhorting mummy and daddy to splash out on such a ridiculous car while behind those pleading eyes the brisk crack of teeth on windscreen played over and over.

My Becky drove no such monstrosity; had she been so inclined she could have screamed for one until her head fell off. I shelled out for a nice hatchback, easy as pie to insure. Ok, so she decked out the inside with a selection of fluffy smiley crap but I must have had inane toys grinning from the dash too when I was her age.

I was never a nervous driver 'til she got her plates.

Suddenly I wanted John, his warm living flesh and never mind what he'd say seeing the red car crumpled up like trash thrown away in the scrub, one indicator still winking steadily. His office remained on quick dial, a throwback to the old days, but as I tilted my aching neck against the headrest my reflection came up too clearly in the rear vision mirror.

I slipped the phone away even as John was saying hello? Hello?

Those good old days were so very far behind us.

IMGR8 boasted the boy's vanity plates. Bet he sat up all night thinking of that one. He had literally flown out of nowhere, in heavy afternoon traffic where the rest of the world had been getting by on life's simple formula: you go then I go. Smooth as cogs and nobody gets burned. Engines droned like drowsy afternoon bees.

Then BANG! The garish penismobile blasted by, half in my lane and then roaring out again, I swear he actually passed through my front fender. Then over the hills and far away, although not too far for me to give chase. One thought burned behind my eyes like magnesium ignited, razing any sensible consideration to the ground.

It could have been Becky.

In my place my Becky with her brave little P plates might have panicked. She might have freaked right out in fact, and ploughed into that green paling fence over there; no Great Wall of China but enough to make a pancake of her white icing car.

Following the boy's thumping bass trail, IMGR8 in my face and his dirty exhaust peeling across my hood my hands couldn't hold the wheel: they were all trembly and wanted to float away. An accident could still happen to Becky. It might be happening right now.

Why oh why didn't we buy her a bigger car? Perhaps a tank.

John's high-speed navigation can be very much like the boy's: he drives, quite frankly, like a jerk. In the pursuit it was all getting jumbled in my adrenaline-stung brain and I saw red everywhere: red lipstick on intimate skin, and perhaps I'd imagined blood in my adversary's teeth even then.

Eventually I found myself sitting outside the boy's house. Flushed with the sudden power of knowing where he lived, but not sure what to do about it. Drumming on the wheel, biting my lip nervously. It could have been Becky.

That first flaming alarm remained as banked coals in my head, waiting, and I hated his smug red car tucked safely in the driveway.

And, well … I guess you can guess the rest: how his car ended up where it did. Not exactly up there with the Earhart mystery, is it?

Thus ran my tearful confession, my song and dance for sympathy to that goody two-shoes smart bitch Amy, who snooped my sedan's telling injuries from all the way across the street.

Amy, Amy, lives on her own. Peeping Amy. Everybody needs good neighbours. Listened to my tale with all the aplomb of an Irish pastor; I understand dear, I do. Patting my head with worm-cold fingers. Exposing horsy teeth in a tannin stained grimace.

White flecks circled in my tea but I steeled myself and sipped because she wasn't running to the papers as she should, in horror and glory.

And next Wednesday there were scrapes of alien green on Amy's front bumper, one headlight cracked right across its face. But of course—there's her boy.

Jackrabbit timid; lives with his pa who'd likely prefer a real son over a little wooden toy but we all work with what we get. It was the father who bullied the lad into his license in the first place.

That Stratton woman's car is taking a beating, John has commented over dinner while sitting back and taking great slurps of wine. Amy, isn't it? Dunno how she manages it.

With a mouthful of minted peas I throw in an obliging titter, but I can't taste a thing, and am having terrible trouble listening to John. Johnny-boy, my husband. Perhaps he's having a dig at the multiplying dints and bingles in my own paintwork.

I can't concentrate with Becky sitting there jangling her keys in her pocket. She has a feathery pink something with goggle eyes on the chain and she won't want dessert, she's impatient to be up from the table and away. The window scrolled down to blow her long gold hair rippling over the seats.

If I could drag my thoughts together, what I would like is to join John under the water after dinner; isn't that what we had the double showerheads installed for? I could just slip in while his back is turned and surprise him, hopefully in a good way.

Instead I'll pack away the dishes and rather forlornly wrap Becky's favourite dessert to pop in the fridge. I can't join John under the shower tonight.

It feels like my Becky's keys are chingling away between my ears.

And let's face it. John drives like a jerk.

Commitment

bp gregory

COMMITMENT

11:00PM. LOVELY TIFFANY CHATTING.

WITH THE PHONE'S smooth plastic nestling cool against her cheek, Tiffany silently debated whether a lonely dark stairwell would be worth finding out what the hell was going on up there. Despite the inner-city chic of it all, sometimes the tawdry drawbacks of studio living could really outweigh the kicks.

'Yeah? Is that so?'

Murmuring through glossy lips Tiffany used that warm lilt a woman only directs to her lover when she wants something. If it weren't for those pale baby-blue orbs turned up to the ceiling, narrowed through their lashes, a watcher might not think her distracted at all.

'Well I'm not going to miss you, sunshine. I'm so not! Come on: you'll be gone for what, two weeks? Three? There's plenty a girl can find to fill in her time over three weeks. Nope, you'll just have to call me. I can't find your number.'

Actually Tiffany had it memorized, but no point making him feel special this early on in the piece. With a lazy arc of the spine she stretched her bare toes and kicked a biro off the bed.

'No I can't find a pen. No point telling me now, I'll never remember it. At least this way I'll know when you phone that you've been thinking of me.'

A tiny smile, unconsciously sensual, warmed the corners of Tiffany's mouth. Now she had what those two were up to up there, she'd bet her life on it. From up above her ceiling came the soft but unmistakable sigh of a couple making love.

They might have been half asleep. Two unthinking bodies wrapped in each other's warmth, turning by instinct to each other in the night. Their bed could even be directly above hers, Tiffany thought dreamily. Her neighbors' twining bodies aligned perfectly with her own as she lounged on the bedspread.

A smudge of lip gloss had found its way onto the bubblegum-grape handset. Tiffany smeared it absently with her thumb.

'What? Oh, the noise: it's the people in two-b at it again. Two-b, upstairs, you know; the flat I applied for first. The one with the view.

'Actually no, I take it back. You can hear my hoards and hoards of lovers crammed into the closet, just begging me to get off the line so the ravishment may begin.

'Now you come to mention it I *was* thinking of going up there or banging on the roof with a broom but then I thought, why should I? Can't say it 'bothers' me, as such.'

Her glossy lips drew the same slow line again, only this time entirely for him.

'Don't you know it, baby. Well . . . maybe I do miss you just that little bit.'

Events upstairs were no longer a peaceful interlude.

Less comfortable now with being proxy to their act Tiffany slid off the bed and began to pace, toenails catching in frayed shag-pile. Her face dropped back into its habitual pout.

A man's heavy breathing began to filter through the thin plaster and a woman's rhythmic gasps; ragged, unconscious of being heard. Towed by its cord the phone clattered off the pillow and followed Tiffany's progress back and forth like an appendage, or an over-eager pet.

'So why didn't you phone earlier? Haven't got someone there, have you?'

Laughter spurted out, as sharp and fleeting as any of her emotions.

'No hon, nobody here either—sorry to disappoint, but no orgy. Well I'm not surprised you can hear it: two-b are rocking the foundations here.'

She stopped musingly in front of the dresser, inhaling from its heavy cargo of talcum, perfume and deodorant. That mirror could sure do with a good clean.

'Do you remember when we used to be like that? I loved how hungry you used to feel back then, like the big bad wolf. You were going to eat me all up. Legs and face and boobs and . . .

'No! Why don't you? I'm not going to say it if you won't.' She laughed. 'Remember the night we celebrated my application for two-b? It was so going to be my perfect home. You were a bit scary but I loved it. I liked you scaring me. I wondered what you were going to do once you'd gobbled me all up and there was nothing left.'

Tiffany's reflection polished its teeth with a short pink tongue.

'When do you plan on coming home? I know it's not exactly two-b down here but I'm sure I can think of some way to welcome you back.'

Her pout sank into discontent, voice rising to a sulky, childlike whine.

'But I want you here, now. Well why not? Why shouldn't you come back home? I don't care. Don't bait me, I *so* don't. Why should two-b be getting all the fun?'

11:42 PM. THE FLYING FACE CREAM.

After a struggle, with fingers bent daintily to protect the nails, Tiffany had finally succeeded in shifting her mirror off the dresser and propping it against the wall.

Now she sat before it with one foot against silvered glass, painting her toenails pomegranate-red. The hand left free toyed restlessly with her hair. In that position Tiffany was a candy fantasy left to her own devices; a divine Monroe engrossed in her super-feminine ritual.

Suddenly a door slammed upstairs, shuddering through the whole building.

Startled, Tiffany dropped the nail polish bottle, but was already too busy listening to notice. Either a bout of really raunchy action was getting underway in two-b, or an absolutely monumental fight. Mixing those two up was not a mistake Tiffany wanted to make. Strange that it would be so hard to tell.

She stood aghast for a moment with one bird-boned hand over her mouth. The voice that slipped past her fingers sounded very small.

'That doesn't sound like fun.'

She took a few uncertain steps to the centre of the room. So little space: two steps and you were out of the bedroom, three steps the kitchen, two the toilet.

It did not sound like fun at all.

'Hello?'

The odds were that two-b couldn't have heard Armageddon over their own racket.

'Hey, you guys had better keep it down.'

The male voice dominated. If anything, the chaos grew louder.

And if there was anything Tiffany was unaccustomed to, it was being ignored.

Lighting first on her cosmetics she began pelting loose objects at the ceiling, anything she could get her hands on. For a smallish girl she had a great arm on her. One cold cream jar left a prominent crater beside the light fitting.

'Hey. Hey! What's going on up there?'

The impromptu missiles rained down on Tiffany and she threw them again and again, the frustrated grinding of her teeth a clamour in her head. The bedroom became choking, suffocating in a cloying mix of spilt make-up and artificial fragrances.

The flat overhead shook with thuds and crashes as things were knocked over and smashed by the grappling pair inside. Then came one louder thump, much louder. Almost, thought Tiffany, as though the woman had been flung, arms flailing, against a wall.

'No! Stop! Stop it, you're hurting her!'

Buried up to her trim ankles in broken objects and trinkets, the previously neat bedroom in instant disarray, Tiffany screeched at the ceiling in impotent rage.

'Stop hurting her!'

The only thing left in place was the purple phone, still on the bed with the orderly puce numbers of its keypad glowing smugly. Ripping the jack free, Tiffany shrieked and hurled that, too. It knocked the light askew and then clattered to the carpet with a faint "bring".

She transferred her frustration to it without missing a beat, savaging her palms with ten perfectly painted fingernails.

'Why don't you ring me, you stupid jerk? What are you doing? Why aren't you here?'

11:55PM. A PRETTY DROP OF SWEAT MEANDERS DOWN TIFFANY'S PALE CHEEK.

There was no longer the slightest suspicion of love play, no confusion. All play and all love in two-b had ceased.

What they were saying was almost impossible to distinguish through the ceiling, although amid raised voices one word could be heard loud and clear from the woman like a gull's cry.

'Don't!'

Tiffany sat cross-legged in the wreckage that had been her bedroom. The telephone she cradled comfortably like a treasured child, its receiver loose in the hand that rested on her thigh. Her blue eyes were squeezed tight by premature lines, kept hidden and safe behind the retreat of her fringe. Dully, she repeated,

'Don't.'

The protest upstairs was muffled silent. It might have been smothered under the rough skin of a large palm, blunt fingernails like shovels wrapping about her jaw. Tiffany could practically taste his sweat on her lips, thick and yeasty.

The man's hard breathing, forced over and through swampy sinuses, was all that remained.

Although the jack lay unplugged and coiled laxly around her feet Tiffany listlessly lifted the phone's handset to her face.

'Remember when we used to be like that?'

As she listened her overlying expression, one of vague disconnection, remained. All but for a single line between her plucked eyebrows which hardened ominously.

'Of course it really happened that way. Does it sound like the sort of thing I'd forget in a hurry?'

She closed her eyes and put her hand over the mouthpiece for a moment, struggling for composure.

'Why are you breathing so hard? Are you angry, is that it? Are you angry with me?'

A flash flood of fury swept Tiffany's very breath away, and on that forehead the line gaped and yawed like a chasm.

'You son of a bitch. Oh, you dirty son of a bitch.'

Her throat contracted to a pinprick, so she could barely speak.

'What right do you have to get mad at me? I'm here all alone dealing with this when you should be here, too; why the hell aren't you here . . . Don't hang up! Don't you dare hang up on me!'

She shrieked furiously and pitched the phone at her own reflection.

'You bastard!'

Tiffany's big mirror tipped and fell with a dull crunch, fracturing into a billion lines. As though in reply the screaming up in two-b renewed with a vengeance, vibrating the windows in their frames. The man was grunting fleshily like an overweight bull ready to charge.

'So that's how it is, huh?'

Tiffany's flushed face turned up, her voice spiralling.

'Not good enough for you, was I? Well, leave her alone, you dirty bastard. I won't let you hurt her, too!'

11:59PM. THE LONELY DARK STAIRWELL.

Crying incoherently Tiffany wrenched open her front door and was swallowed by the stairwell's darkness. The steps burnt her bare feet like dry ice.

'Stop hurting her!'

12:00AM. TIFFANY HAS SPENT ONE HOUR ON HER OWN.

How could this be?

Tiffany's skin was hot, so burning that the tears practically sizzled off her cheeks. Her head ached and throbbed from crying; she felt dizzy and sick. Enveloped in a fever nightmare she burst from the cold stairwell through the open front door, into the warm light of flat two-b.

But this was her flat.

Tiffany twisted to look uncertainly back at the stairs she had climbed (feeling a pinging in her spine), then about her again. Her dresser mirror lay exhausted and crazed on the floor. The grape phone squatted upright on it, at the centre of a complex series of impact fissures, like a spider in its web. Tiffany's own footprints in spilt pomegranate nail polish ran everywhere, out the door and then back in again. It was dead silent. There was nobody here.

In fact, the only thing missing from Tiffany's home was Tiffany herself. So she came right in and shut the door, two-b on the shiny bronze plaque, behind her.

She had to step delicately like a wading heron to avoid all the broken junk on the floor. Luckily the phone jack, although a little bent, had survived its rough treatment. Tiffany blew on it, and then with a bit of wiggling managed to plug it back into the wall.

Wiping her sore eyes and nose on her sleeve, Tiffany cleared some floor space with her foot. Then she sat down in the room she'd created and dialled a phone number.

'Samuel? Are you there hon?'

From the Author

A little about the story:
Commitment evolved out of many evenings in a thin walled apartment, chewing old grievances and obsessions until they assumed gruesome proportions.

People can go a little mad when left on their own. When first your mind and then reality refuse to co-operate with your desires, what then?

THE MAN'S HEART

BP GREGORY

A SHORT STORY

THE MAN'S HEART

THE MAN'S TIME was set out for him before he was the man, or even the boy. In those first moments when he was simply *the embryo*, silicate wires and clockwork pieces were inserted into the tiny beginnings of his heart. They were there when the butterfly fluttering of cells coalesced into the first coherent thump, and for every beat afterwards. His allotted heartbeats had begun.

The device ensured a certain, precisely measured passage between the beats—no more, no less. Surge as the hormonal sea might from his endocrine system, it would never put its passionate strain on his heart. Every day commenced with a numbered beat that had been pre-ordained before even he was.

That wired muscle behind his ribcage pulsed to the rhythm of every human chest on the planet. A magnificent, perfectly timed symphony. Barring accident, two men born at the same time were given the same slice from the pie of life to do with what they may.

A counter in the man's pocket kept the beat, a birthday gift from his parents. Wrought-brass on a polished chain, with his name engraved in ornate curling letters inside the casing. When nervous he would flick it open and closed in the palm of his hand.

Through the counter the man knew when all the major events of his life were scheduled; it had all been arranged, so he could attain everything society dictates a happy person should have.

For instance, at *this many beats* he was to attend a job interview. The interviewers' own heartbeats told them when to expect him. At *this many beats* he was due to go clubbing with his friends. At *this many beats* he would marry, and at *this many beats* he would father his first child. Time marched to the beats of his heart, the steps ordered and regular.

The man was there when his father's allotment was up. It was nothing like the random years, when uncertain life could drop out from under you at any moment. The man's father had known. He wound up his job. He paid all his bills. He spent a decent amount of beats with his family, calm and prepared, and died peacefully on an idyllic hillside where he had loved to watch the ocean.

With the saline wind shaking his hair, the man had put his hand onto his father's broad chest to feel the heart stop. It happened between moments, with no faltering; the device remained working right up to the end. The next heartbeat was just not there.

Thanks to the counter, the man knew how many beats away his own end was. Sometimes he dreamed that as his last moments measured out, a giant painted-tin toy rat came and stuck its own key into his heart, winding him up. Sometimes

THE MAN'S HEART

he dreamed that his chest was in fact a giant pendulum clock, sweeping away the hours. The man dreamed of many things, but he could afford to. The day his heart would stop was still *so many beats* away.

From the Author

A little about the story:
The Man's Heart is an incredibly early piece of flash fiction, stemming right back to the art festivals my high school was so fond of throwing around. For this particular event, the chosen theme was "Time," and the permitted word count constricting. I began by thinking about what people's relationship to time was.

I'd been particularly fascinated during that period by my father's brief snippets and tales of his relationship with *his* father: according to my youthful, sketchy understanding a rather cold, distant English figure who did right by his family by working himself into an early grave. A greater contrast to my own vibrant, humorous father with his close ties to his hero-worshiping kids couldn't be found.

So, within the tight confines of the given word limit I banged out *The Man's Heart*, and it got picked up to be read at assembly. Painfully shy in my awful bowl haircut I demurred doing the deed myself, and they chose one of the handsomely groomed theatre-class kids at random to take up the duty instead.

Right from the first word mumbled into the microphone, it became brutally clear the poor guy hadn't even skimmed the text before getting up. He had no sense of the tale's rhythm, jerking and pausing painfully in all the wrong places like a high-camp Shatner monologue. Any sense of meaning got utterly lost, and you could see his eyes screw up in confusion at each line, wondering what the sod was this next bit?

I believe I was the only one in that entire packed hall who enjoyed a second of it. The story's continuity had been broken into disparate fragments of time, which spun and glittered in the air entirely independent of each other, like some nonsensical piece of modern art.

A few people came up to me afterward to ask "What the hell?" And all I could do was shake my head ruefully and say, "I loved it."

This was also the time I was fermenting the concepts that would eventually lead to the novel Automatons, and you can taste fleshy humanity's envy of the neat clockwork life in *The Man's Heart*.

It's All About The LOVE

BP GREGORY

IT'S ALL ABOUT THE LOVE

FATTY GOLDEN OIL crackled and popped while Boris Bulgaris, who was supposed to be watching the fries, pensively pulled a long strip of skin from his lip and stared off into space. The air was heavy with greased molecules that lubricated the airways and lungs with every breath. Boris loved this place. God, he loved it.

"BORRY!" Pannager the Manager's abrasive haemorrhoidal bellow cut abruptly through the larger man's pleasant reflections. The Manager himself popped into view: poster boy for the customer-service generation, utterly smoothed and groomed to perfection.

"Yeah?" Now where did that bit of skin go?

"You are *supposed* to be *watching* those chips, not fantasizing about porking them rotten! Now get that soggy three-chinned butt in gear and batter up another chunk'o'chicken, people are *hungry!*"

That was how Pannager actually spoke; with so many italics you'd think he was forcing a turd. Which was funny because that was just how he looked, too.

Boris' watered jelly eyes narrowed to bitter slits, squeezing gluey beeswax from their corners like butter through a salada. Pannager didn't deserve to be in charge here. He just did not *get it* (to borrow some of the man's own inflection).

The simple beauty of the whole fried-food phenomena was lost on him. To Pannager, the fluorescent-baked wonderland was merely his own little dictatorship, a tiny dribble of power to compensate for the handicap of his abnormally shrivelled, monkey-like genitals. Yes indeed, Boris had actually caught the famous Manager with his pressed pants down and his tool out one afternoon, indulging in a touch of literature in the dusty urine-scented venue of the broom closet. Pannager had never forgiven Boris for discovering what wiggled ashamedly 'round in his trousers.

Little (ha-ha) Boris cared. What he knew was that he had been born for this place in the way that some were meant for greatness. Here, and only here did Boris' scabrous skin glow with true health, and rare prehistoric butterflies of beauty lumbered through his swampland mind. Beneath the sterile eye-searing light that strangled normal conversations at their birth, leaving customers sitting numbly around a plastic tabletop, Boris' imagination spouted glorious reverent poetry to the wonder of food.

He had always worked with food. Chicken-boner, abattoir-hacker, biscuit-packer; always searching for . . . he didn't know what. Some elusive element, unknown but as instinctive as migration. Then one day in a drive-thru it finally came to Boris, the great and eternal truth of life. Fast food was made with love.

To hell with vitamin enhanced frozen meals and their quarantined plastic wrapped Laura Palmer lives. The thick plop of hunks of naked pink chicken dropping into the fryer filled his heart with cholesterol-clogged joy. Burger patties sizzling and extruding on the grill made his head swim. Boxes of onion . . .

"BULGIE!" Pannager the Manager screamed in impotent choirboy rage right behind him. "Stop wet dreaming! Work or get *out!*"

Boris Bulgaris did not even think. He simply seized Pannager the Manager by the roots of his carefully coiffured hair (the regulation hairnet yielded a surprisingly firm grip) and thrust his obnoxious head firmly into the bubbling volcano of the fryer.

Oil snarled viciously, but although thousands of new eruptions shook the surface of the liquid Pannager himself was making no audible sounds—it were as though the fryer raged for him. Or perhaps, Boris thought musingly, it was because his prissy little lips were kissing the element at the bottom. Long crispy strips of skin began boiling to the surface.

The noble Pannager was not taking this new development calmly. His pale freckled limbs flailed frantically in spastic throes, but as his anal-efficiency kept the kitchen regulation tidy there was nothing to knock over, nothing to seize. In the extremes of agony one elbow broke itself with an audible 'crack', needling the skin with splinters of bone from the inside out.

More skin, golden delicious looking shreds. Their appearance gradually filtered through to Boris and when inspiration dawned (slowly, daybreak was always gradual in this part of the world) he giggled and snorted. A long horsy stream of mucus rocketed back through his nasal cavity at ballistic speed to spatter on the jiving lobes of his forebrain.

The next morning there was a new nameplate under the sign 'Store Manager', polished as bright and shiny as a new dollar. Manager Boris Bulgaris stood demurely behind the counter, and such was the height that nobody could tell he had no pants on. His thick drooping dick: bigger than a baby's arm, more like the whole infant—no resemblance to the late Pannager there—pressed reassuringly against the cool dial of the safe.

So long as the money kept rolling in to head office there was nothing Boris couldn't do. For instance, nobody knew how he had laved his body in warm mashed potato and gravy last night—oh joyous, he'd been waiting to do that since day one.

But most, oh yes most importantly no customer would question why their 'chicken' suddenly had freckles. Boris was really going to have to advertise for new employees—fresh meat, as the case may be.

Manager Boris scratched his foreskin complacently on the stainless steel, dislodging cheesy flakes that had been trapped under the fold. New menu specials, ice-creams, drinks: there was forever to experiment.

God, how he loved this job.

THE ELEVATOR STORY

BP GREGORY

THE ELEVATOR STORY

THE LADY WASN'T going to make the elevator.

She burst down the corridor, heels striking click-click and a shoulder thrust through elevator doors that shut regardless. Jim flinched but of course the mechanical horrors you read about are one in a million; the doors swept back again and released her just as mindlessly as the vice had closed. Where he would have been freaked she was already purse-rummaging, not to squander a moment.

Air whuffed as the doors sealed, restoring pressurised calm. Lavender in the confines—that had to be the lady. Jim's royal bitch of a heavy parcel grew heavier as dim numbers started ticking up, and he shifted uncomfortably. He'd be glad to be rid of it.

You wouldn't read about *this*: the lady was boldly checking his reflection in her compact, even as he looked her over. Jim would set her at forty to a day and precisely turned out, making the best of what the brood mares squandered. Haughty to boot! Jim's lips quirked when deft fingers dismissively snapped the compact away: well, we aren't all born on the road to glory. At least with deliveries, all the cycling left him with a butt that squeaked when he walked.

No chops for the meat in the sandwich, their glacial third fellow in broadsheet cuffs. Suit by the house of what every fucking guy's wearing. Jim's full hands at least tendered some excuse for not holding the door for the lady, but the suit had blanked the entire human population and any obligation to them off the skin of the earth.

Suit stared up at the numbers with wide blind eyes. Between them they carved the elevator's space into a trinity so inviolate it was a while before anybody managed to notice that the damned thing had stopped.

Realisation slowly spread, and sidled into awkwardness, until somebody had to say something.

And that somebody was always Jim. He shot the lady a wry shrug. 'Don't you hate that?'

'Only ever happens when you're busting.' She responded, rounded caramel tones pegging him as a graceless hick.

But a hick with tenacity, damnit. 'It's done this before?'

'Handful of times. Never with folk in it, though; they prise the doors open to check. You look a little peaky.'

'For those of us not fond of technology the world is an unkind place.'

'Speaking of,' she murmured in an undertone. Their marginalised third had set about mashing the elevator buttons at random. Uninvited, the lady leaned in with exaggerated patience. 'This one here's the intercom.'

Suit intercepted her reach to jab the button a half dozen impatient times, hard enough to rattle plastic. No doubt about it: there would be a thunderbolt stroke at the end of this fellow's corporate rainbow.

Steel twanged ominously in the shaft outside and Jim's glands irised open, broadcasting his nervousness rather embarrassingly to whoever cared to sniff in the confined space.

Which was nothing compared to what happened next.

Sudden garble erupted from the grille. Modern chaos with a slow yawing groan. Just as suddenly, the courier's tense stink was no longer alone.

Stubbornly refusing to concede to fate, Suit bent to the speaker. 'Hello? Is anyone getting me?'

Jim could well imagine the thick listening silence at the other end and wanted to warn Suit to get his face away from it, but his less theatrical partner ventured, 'Shouldn't you press when you talk?'

Suit glared around but there was nothing for it now. They existed. He pushed the button. 'Hello?'

What spewed out was deafening; their listener must have twisted the dial all the way. Jim found himself stammering absurdly, 'Don't—don't tell it we're here …' But of course, nobody would ever be told. Pain mewled in his skull. The sound was drilling straight through his eye sockets.

'Hey! Hey the elevator's stopped. Come get us!'

A long thoughtful hiss.

Then the speaker clicked off. The sudden tension rang like being struck deaf and the lady slowly took her hands down from her ears.

'Piece of shit,' Suit snorted truculently.

Fool of subtlety, Jim took that moment to burst the silence with a gargantuan sneeze. It went off like Fat Boy in the confines, anointing the wall where some vandal had scratched GATE in brutal semi-literate glyphs. The lady shrieked in disgust and then stood trembling with knees squeezed. Jim had just tested her pelvic resolve in a big way.

Of course Suit had an opinion. 'You know, back in the old country we'd cover our mouth.'

'Sorry. Caught me by ...' "Surprise" got blown to shreds but at least he got a hand up this time, wiping it rather shamefacedly on his trousers. 'Doesn't anyone have a mobile?' Jim thought of claiming his own as busted, but why gussie the truth with these two? 'My provider had some issue with non-payment.'

Suit crossed his arms. 'Don't have one.'

'Really?'

Suit had genuinely startled the others, and they seemed to demand an explanation. 'Don't want clients thinking they can reach me anytime.'

'Like now, huh?' Jim set his parcel down carefully, leaning on the wall. 'I never met anyone who didn't *want* a phone. My niece has one and she's *nine*.'

'Pays her bill, does she?'

'Well … What do you do when stuff goes wrong?'

'Like now, huh?' Suit sneered. 'I suppose I'd just borrow one.'

'So really your freedom comes at the expense of those around you.'

Suit turned a martyred grimace on the lady. 'Ma'am, may I use your phone?'

'I've not been in the habit of bringing it on the thrilling trip to the ladies.' Her eyes flickered uncomfortably. 'Doubtless I will in future. Are we totally stuffed? Shouldn't a courier have a radio?'

'*Legit* ones get all sorts of fancy junk. I took bookings via text for a while; now without a phone …' Jim shrugged. 'Being late with this today isn't gonna help. Probably cost me the work.' He closed his eyes and slid wearily down the wall to sit on the parcel.

'Jesus.' The lady wrinkled her nose and he shrugged.

'It's only a job. Plenty more in the sea.'

'Only if you've got a big rod,' Suit threw in with uncharacteristic humour but the lady refused to be charmed.

'If you want to avoid a sea in here we'd better get ourselves out.'

'Hey.'

Jim's eyes cracked open; Suit was peering down at him.

'You ok?'

'Not great,' he admitted. 'I've been staving off this flu all week. Felt alright until,' he flapped a hand at the speaker grille, 'The noise.'

'That's awesome.' The lady was spooked like a strung filly. 'I don't need to be catching your germs either.'

'You heard the lady.' Suit clapped Jim chummily on the shoulder. What a butthead. 'Let's try busting those doors open.'

Jim just sort of feebly hung off his side of the door more than helping. He felt like cooked spaghetti; *hard done by* spaghetti which didn't incline him to apply. The lady would have managed far better, but she had already been gender pigeonholed. Just stood by in time-honoured fashion, fiddling with her handbag.

'A trifle weird don't you think?' She observed nervously, to be participating. 'Three grown adults cut off from the world and the elevator just happens to stop.'

Jim laughed breathlessly. 'Karmic?'

'Balls,' Suit grunted. 'You said it stops all the damned time.'

'I mean, I feel like anything might happen. Because we're isolated.'

'Two blokes and you're what, five-nine in heels? Hardly babes in the wood.'

She flushed. Breathless femininity was not going well. 'It sounds paranoid out loud ... and really we're no less *capable* without phones.'

'Except we can't call for help.' The prospect had Suit more

smug than dismayed. She made one last effort to rally.

'I mean in our own resources.'

'You never know,' Jim wheezed. 'Maybe catching a few of us away from the herd would be too delicious for fate to miss.'

'Predetermination can kiss my ...' With a gasp of depressurisation the doors scrolled reluctantly apart.'

'Hell,' Suit finished in disgust.'

The elevator's light flickered over a solid and forbidding cinderblock wall, with GATE slashed across it in faded yellow paint. Their friend the omnipresent tagger had made his way here, too.

The lady disbelievingly laid one manicured hand on the wall but its density left no room for doubt. Further, the blocks seemed to radiate a dim antiquity that left her feeling grey. Grey, like windowless offices and Christmas alone.

'It's cold!' She jerkily tried to rub pink life back into the fingers. 'What were our chances of getting stuck right between floors?'

'Probably ...' Suit started but Jim sneezed again, explosively, losing his grip on the door and what splattered the cinderblock was a lavish sacrificial red.

The lady wailed like an air raid, flailing away so that although Suit yelled, 'Oh, oh Jesus!' it was up to him to catch Jim as the lad buckled. The doors slid back together, complicitly hiding the mess as though things were just dandy folks. Fine, but for Jim's dripping nostrils and chin.

'Shit! Oh Shit!' Their maiden held forth hysterically as Suit lowered Jim to the floor. 'What's wrong with him!'

'Just a cold really ...' Jim bubbled, his eyes like swollen cherries.

'Oh Christ he's like ice! Will you shut it and get over here to help please?'

With a high horrified whine the lady pressed further into

the corner and then an unmistakable reek spilled into the air. Six glasses of lunchtime sauvignon blanc as strained through the human uric system.

With hands over her face she began to cry, humiliated heaves falling thin and hollow in the reeking air.

'Oh jeeze.'

She couldn't even stand to look at them through her fingers.

Breathing through his mouth Suit set to mopping Jim's face with his tie, in motions surprisingly competent and gentle. And after a few minutes of not being the sole tragedy the lady's sobs hiccupped, then slowed.

When she finally spoke, although tremulous her voice was brittle with assumed dignity. 'Would you please turn around? My stockings are wet. I'd like to take them off.'

Suit kept up the good work, and while Jim couldn't twist away entirely he put his face to the wall and stared fixedly at GATE.

There was an inelegant splat of underthings and then she coughed. 'Stinks. Sorry.'

'You wouldn't have pissed yourself if you could help it,' Suit dismissed her brusquely and added his tie to the pile. 'Just call this laundry corner.'

She knelt into Jim's field of view although notably not too close, mouth an ill-humoured line. 'Just what the hell's happening?'

'Don't feel so bad now.' The courier spat, a gory Rorschach, and tried to smile at her. His gums were a nightmare. 'Just a cold. Didn't mean to scare anybody.'

'Balls to that!' Suit stood. 'He needs a hospital, like now. There's a way up top—come help me here.'

Lacking strength of arm the lady made a step of her bare knee—even so the ceiling hatch was almost beyond them. Finally, wobbling between her support and the wall Suit managed to pop the access, letting in a burst of arctic air from the shaft.

It felt old, full of machinery, and whipped the lady's ordered hair about her narrow triangle of a face. On the floor Jim shivered and groaned, trying his best to roll up like a pill bug. 'You sure you ought to be going up there?'

'Well we certainly don't have all day to dick around in here.'

Suit had found purchase somewhere and was slowly levering his way up into the dark by brute determination when the lady went crashing back against the wall, her eyes bugging from her head an a way that put the right horrors up Jim.

Breath whistling he uncurled as far as he could but their confined little world had gone all red and curdled. He just couldn't see.

'Where did he go? Is he up there?'

'I DIDN'T SEE!' she shrieked, spit flying and blanched fingertips clawing right in her mouth. Her bare legs pinwheeled and squeaked against the floor. 'I DIDN'T SEE ANYTHING, DON'T ASK MEEEE!'

'Hey. Hey lady, stop.' Jim hitched himself painfully into the dimness of her chosen corner and tried to administer comforting pats, except that what he raised seemed to be a mushy ball at the end of his wrist. No fingers. It thudded impotently off her shoulder and probably wasn't very reassuring. 'Stop freaking out. It's gonna be ok.'

There was a muted thumping from outside the elevator as though some heaviness was banging along the exterior. A rattling at the doors and the lady gagged, trying literally to shove herself through the wall.

'What's that?' Jim croaked, peering. Warm pink fluid ran down his cheeks. 'Is that him?'

' … I didn't, don't let it in, I didn't see …'

THE ELEVATOR STORY

The doors juddered open, forced by two chapped hands and a squarish man stood blinking in the opening. He had the no-nonsense build of a tradesman, a fellow driving the pragmatic middle of life's highway with reigns firmly in hand.

'Hey!' The tradie yelled down the gap into the elevator shaft below, squatting a little. 'Hey, reckon you've had vandals in here!'

'That's awesome. Gimme some more showstoppers.' The grumbling reply came from much further down, several floors, jostled by echoes up the shaft but partaking in the same sane heartiness. 'The magnet isn't reaching. I'm going t' have to get down in the bottom of the shaft.'

Tradie scratched his sparse hair, sighed. 'You want me to come down?'

A thin torch beam lanced accusingly up through the gap at him, swirling motes disturbed by all the shouting. 'You stay right where you are like your feet are nailed down! We wouldn't even be here if some Einstein hadn't figured on dropping his keys down the shaft, and that elevator's one fucking tetchy bitch. If she comes down on my skull I'll be right back to haunt you!'

'Fine, fine.'

Tradie's eye wandered idly about the elevator interior. Really, when it came to mess the kids who got into these buildings were worse than vermin. He chuckled deep in his throat: damn pity you couldn't bait for them in the same way.

The elevator stank of old piss, and a tangle of rubbish had been dumped for the next schmo to have to clean. God even knew what that pink foam was; slowly eating its way down into the floor with the faintest of crackling noises. A flattened box and what looked like shreds of lycra were melted in. That'd be a solvent job for sure.

He tried to smudge the word GATE away but some little

bugger had scratched it into the wall with something sharp. Even the ceiling hatch was sprung, a solid block of night above his head. Serve the mongrels right if they'd poked the wrong whoosit and sent themselves on the long fall.

Tradie was just hooking a chair in from the lobby so he could reach up when a horrifying squeal rang up the shaft. 'What was that?' he yelled, chewing his lip fit to abandon post. It was the sort of shrillness that put a fellow in mind of rural abattoirs: rows of bled carcasses, old straw and cold steel. Thank goodness he couldn't claim much more imagination than that.

'Hey! Hey, there's some lady down here!'

'What, in the *elevator* well?' Digging in his ear didn't make the news more credible. 'She drunk? Or homeless?' Probably both. Lucky not to have been squashed flat as a tack, give the cleaners some major overtime to deal with.

'I don't bloody well know, do I? There's—something wrong with her, I don't know. Look, I'm getting her out. Give me twenty to clear the shaft and then I want your fat ass on the horn to the fuzz, the paras, the works, got it?'

'Hey—did you ..?'

'I've got your damned keys!' The voice cracked; any man's reasonable limits would be pushed. 'Just be ready on that phone!'

Something else listened to the excited voices booming up and down the shaft. A thing mashed and spread across the top of the elevator like wet jam, as though smashed from an incredible height.

Impossible that anything like that could still live. Still struggle. Nothing was connected to anything anymore.

But a peeled iris glistened. Fingers quivered and scratched at broadsheet cuffs in a paroxysm of frustration.

There was no real breath behind it so unsurprisingly the man in the elevator failed to hear Suit croaking for help. Instead

THE ELEVATOR STORY

Tradie hopped up on his chair almost as an afterthought, and he popped the ceiling hatch closed.

If you enjoyed these, please read on for special bonus short story Abstract.

ABSTRACT

Whoo a gust of foetid breath puffed from the gaping city loop tunnel to swirl and disperse about the larger space, pushed by what was coming. Definitely a bit of morning whiff, that, not midnight breath. An *"all the beer's dry an' me toothbrush's arsed"* aroma. Just enough to make Randal gag quietly into his cupped palm. Faint and sick.

Desperate for a wee, too. Too much coffee. Meanwhile his inflamed eyes went all around, checking, assessing. Picking nervously at a subterranean claustrophobia. Paranoid his solid paunch was expanding to fill the subway.

It was dread, you see. Pure skin peeling dread and Randal needed to be brave like he'd never been.

No strangers graced the platform. Like fate. Obviously in this day and age with nobody's word worth much there'd be cameras, but how would they identify him snugged up in a hoodie like any unkempt junkie?

Made our Randal appear, or more so, the sort of fellow nice ladies crossed the street to avoid. God help him he did love to see 'em scurry, frail ankles flashing like bunny tails. Didn't make one *feel* any nicer but something was something, hey?

Not five steps and turned away into the wind Broncs had obligingly worn a brimmed hat, hiding his own collapsed face. Fate indeed. Broncs only ventured abroad after dark when there were few to witness. Tantalisingly suspicious … but still, *Old Folk Need Less Zs* the literature claimed, or at least the digital abstracts that were free to read.

Well lucky fucking him. Randal scowled, rubbing at eggplant varicose. He was eternally flattening out beneath exhaustion. His arms and legs weren't proper limbs but weighed as numb kettlebells, had to be lugged about.

He usually lost Broncs after the first hour. Not paying enough mind. Mind, *you* try monitoring the shufflings of a tortoise about town without resting your throbbing brain a second, and doing it dressed as some prat kid besides.

But the online data proved anaemic, no matter how diligently massaged. Eventually he'd been forced to dog those hesitant aged steps, which he liked a lot less.

Randal did wonder if anybody was likely to access his notes someday, read the hints so painstakingly scraped together. He thought not. Not having watched his landlord indiscriminately heaving the previous tenant's belongings to the dumpster out back of the block.

When he'd asked where his predecessor had got to, got a disinterested shrug. Junk. That's all they were. Thousands more where they crept from. Not contributing. Hey, not even procreating; wasn't like any woman in her right mind'd touch 'em.

ABSTRACT

Well, Randal thought, breathing hard, getting a bit excited. He was bloody contributing now!

It had only slowly dawned that he was in fact subsisting in a flat beneath General Fucking Broncawei. But once it had, every creak and shudder of the ceiling became especially ominous.

The light began to flicker in the dim brown haze of Randal's thoughts on the twentieth anniversary of the trials. The photographs got paraded about that time every year, exhorting the public, *"War Criminals Still at Large!"* Only to a world that had already wearied, moved on. Likely what the old bugger was counting on.

An atrocity from the dawn of time, almost before Randal was born. In a place nobody of these parts spared a blink for, even when it had gone up in flames. Why should they? They had movies and shops and chips with friends on the beach. Hot sun and shell grit in their smiling teeth.

Only somebody lacking those gifts would notice.

One hundred and fifty, that's what he'd read. People would only ever care about a hundred fifty others out of the population of the world; because once upon an age that was the size of your standard tribe.

Randal's boss had thought him quite the la di dah for trotting out that gem in the loading dock. The attention was nice, although in the abstract he never managed to dig into the nuts and bolts of anything, never understood *why*.

'You and me, old man,' he muttered at the humped back while gusts of air grew fierce. 'You're my hundred fifty.'

A part of Randal was already looking forward to getting this over with. Psyching himself up had left him sick all week: squats on the loo best not mentioned, the flat viewed through a sort of headachy nausea. He had promised himself a quiet eve with a pizza after.

Numbnuts, he chided, jittery. *Then what'll you do?* Old Broncs was all that got him out of bed of a morning.

Two more anniversaries had dragged by already while he dithered. But this was the third. It'd all gone on too long, right? And he was *quite* sure. *Mostly* sure. Felt the truth, he did, in the cockles of his heart.

General Broncawei. The fucking bogeyman. Why ought humble Randal of all folk to care? Truly he didn't give two short shits what that wheezing, coughing old fart had done in his heyday, although doubtful you got on the news like that for being a saint.

Nope. Randal was knee deep in this, wiping sweaty palms on his leg because *Randal* had never been allowed to get away with any damned thing. Not once in his life.

The sort of existence that made a grown fellow wonder *this isn't at all what I was promised, now. How did this happen?* Nothing but job, rent, washing, chores … he frequently and fervently wished he didn't have to bother his weary skull on it any more.

Stop bothering, then. Purity of the hunt and all that. This was Randal's moment, his big one and wouldn't likely come another. Make it last.

The steely wail of the incoming train. *Dopplered*, that was it, 'though he couldn't recall how it worked.

It was now. Randal tugged the cords of his hoodie for luck, sneakers silent on the platform's pebbled surface—sneaking, ha! Arms outstretched rigid to push. Flabby, that, throw your weight behind it son. Make it count for something.

He stumbled; oh Randal you've fucked it up! Momentum thrusting him on. And there was shrieking, brakes, all the world shrieking, pots and pans and cymbals pummelling his ears. In the throes of it all an iron-hard hand locked onto his arm.

How ironic. Broncs was going to save him.

ABSTRACT

To the old bastard plump Randal must have seemed to spring out of nowhere. So was it mere startlement that made the General's seamed lips, so close as Randal swooped by, seem to peel back in feral satisfaction?

Fresh impetus as the hand thrust him forth. Sudden and shocking.

Last but not least whimpered a plaintive thought in the dark of the tunnel:

… but I'm s'posed to be a hero?

Ha. No time to bother about that anymore.

Also by BP Gregory

Novels

Flora & Jim

The Town

Something for Everything (Automatons Book #2)

Automatons (Automatons Book #1)

Outermen

Novella

Only Skin

Short Story Collections

Orotund, Collected Short Stories Volume Two

Cacophony, Collected Short Stories Volume One

Vu Ja De, Collected Short Stories Volume Three

Kate knows what she saw: a burned out ruin. But the evidence is gone, and nobody else believes the town was ever there.

She knows the town exists. Determined to prove it at any cost, in poking around the outback Kate risks exposing herself and her friends to the slew of horrible urban legends, reticent locals, and too many people who vanished over the years with nowhere to go.

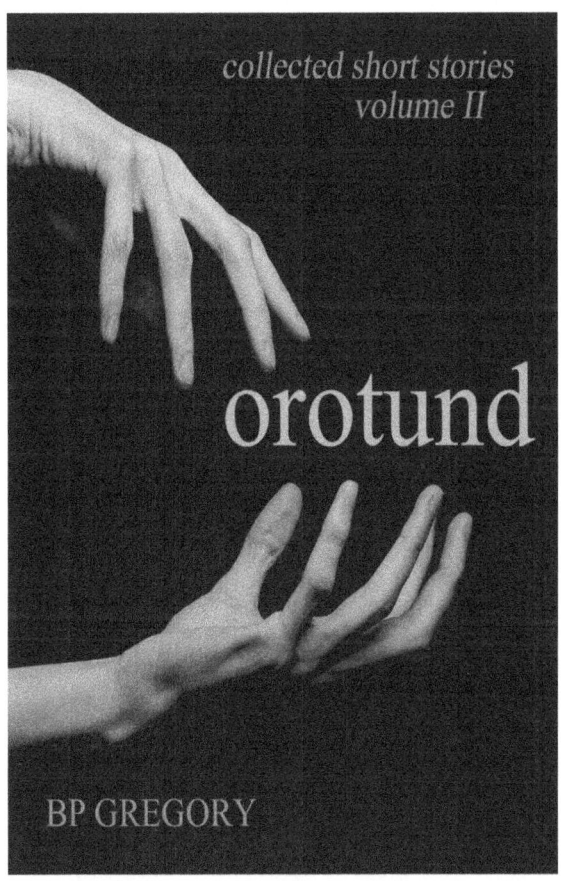

A paroled monster, a prostitute and a policeman all see a little girl lost, but this isn't the start of a joke. An isolated, frail old man trapped in his apartment; what possible threat could he pose to the sociopaths next door?

Take time for a stroll down humanity's eerie back alleys and enjoy BP Gregory's newest short science fiction, urban fantasy and horror stories neatly packaged together in Orotund: Collected Short Stories Volume Two.

SOMETHING FOR EVERYTHING
Automatons Book Two

BP GREGORY

Long ago humanity retreated into migrating cities, leaving the landscape to monsters. Within the safety of walls the caste of Surgeons are denied human touch to preserve their skills.

A Surgeon must not be touched. The city can never stop. Comforting truths to live by. But the other cities have fallen silent. Fear stalks the streets. And John the Surgeon craves touch more than anything.

Monsters, machines and roaming cities, insanity, betrayal and lust: centuries later, the seeds of grim legacy sown in Automatons have borne strange fruit indeed...

Author and avid reader BP Gregory brings monsters, machines and roaming cities, insanity, betrayal and lust! With such tales you shouldn't always feel comfortable or safe.

For sneak peeks, more stories, reviews and recommendations as she ploughs through her to-read pile visit bpgregory.com.

www.ingramcontent.com/pod-product-compliance
Lightning Source LLC
LaVergne TN
LVHW012010260326
834688LV00058B/633